For Jane O'Donoghue
N.J.

First published 1990 by
Walker Books Ltd, 87 Vauxhall Walk
London SE11 5HJ

Text © 1990 Fox Busters Limited
Illustrations © 1990 Norman Johnson

First printed 1990
Printed by South China Printing Co., Hong Kong (1988) Limited

British Library Cataloguing in Publication Data
The whistling piglet.
I. Title
II. Johnson, Norman, *1953-*
823'.914[J]

ISBN 0-7445-1058-9

THE WHISTLING PIGLET

WRITTEN BY
DICK KING-SMITH

ILLUSTRATED BY
NORMAN JOHNSON

WALKER BOOKS
LONDON

"Who's that whistling?" said Mumpig.
"What an awful noise!"

"It's Henry," said nine of her ten spotty piglets.

Henry, the tenth piglet, didn't say anything
because he was busy whistling. He
pursed up his little mouth and
whistled like a blackbird.

"And it's not an awful noise!" cried his brothers and sisters. "It's brill! It's catchy! It makes your feet itch!" and they all began to dance round Henry.

"How shameful!" grunted Mumpig.
"To think that I am the mother of the
world's first whistling piglet!"

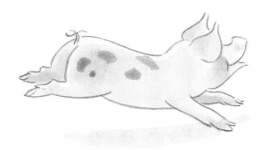

And she was not the only mother on the farm
who did not like what Henry was doing.
"Who's that whistling?" mooed the cows. "What a
fearful row!"

"Who's that whistling?" bleated the sheep. "What a
dreadful din!"

"Who's that whistling?" cackled the hens. "What a
frightful racket!"

But their young ones did not agree.
"It's not a fearful row!" cried the calves and, "It's
not a dreadful din!" cried the lambs and, "It's not
a frightful racket!" cried the baby chicks.
And they all of them said, "It's brill! It's catchy! It
makes your feet itch!" and they all began to dance.

As well as being brill and catchy and making their feet itch, there was one particular tune that Henry sometimes whistled that made all the young animals feel that they would run after him, wherever he went. It was the tune of the song whose words go like this:

Come follow, follow, follow,
Follow, follow, follow me.

Whither shall I follow, follow, follow,
Whither shall I follow, follow thee?

To the greenwood, to the greenwood,
To the greenwood, greenwood tree.

Every time Henry whistled that tune, the calves would break out of their pens; and the lambs would jump out of their fields; and the chicks would flutter out of their runs; and all would rush to follow Henry.

How angry the farmer was!
Almost every day he had to catch all the young
animals and put them back in their proper places.

"And all because of that whistling piglet!" he said to his wife and his little daughter, "What a horrible hullabaloo!"

"It is!" said his wife.
"It's not!" said his little daughter.
"It's brill! It's catchy! It makes your feet itch!"

"They won't itch much longer," said the farmer. "I'm sending him to market next Friday."

Next Friday a lorry came to the farm and drew
up outside Mumpig's sty.
"What's that for, Mumpig?" asked nine of her ten
spotty piglets.
Henry didn't ask because he was busy whistling.
"It's to take you to market."
"What happens there?" they said.

"Someone will buy you and fatten you up,"
said Mumpig.
Henry stopped whistling. "What for?" he said.
"Never you mind," said Mumpig. "Don't bother
your head about that. Just get in the lorry."
But Henry did bother his head. He did
not think that this little piggy wanted
to go to market.

He waited until the sty door was opened and then he began to whistle the tune of the song whose words go like this:

Come follow, follow, follow,
Follow, follow, follow me.

Whither shall I follow, follow, follow,
Whither shall I follow, follow thee?

To the greenwood, to the greenwood,
To the greenwood, greenwood tree.

And he ran as fast as he could, whistling as loud as he could,

past the lorry and across the farmyard
and out into the fields
and away to the greenwood.

And after him ran his nine brothers and sisters.
And after them the calves came galloping, and the lambs
came gambolling, and the chicks came fluttering …

all following the sound of that one particular tune
that made them feel that wherever the whistling
piglet went, there they would go too.

What a business it was for the farmer and
his men to catch them all again!
But calves and lambs are not really happy
in the depths of a wood
(there's not enough grass),
and nor are chicks
(there are too many foxes),
and at last they caught
them all and took them
back to the farm.

The piglets, though, were a different matter, for pigs love woods that are full of acorns and beech-mast and fungi and other lovely things to eat.
So it took the farmer and his men a long time to catch nine of Mumpig's ten spotty children.

The tenth one they never caught.
They searched the greenwood for weeks
and weeks, but they saw nothing.
All they heard—now and again—was the
sound of someone whistling.